THE
BOWLEGGED
ROOSTER

This book belongs to

JOHN

THE BOWLEGGED ROOSTER

*And Other Tales
That Signify*

By Joyce Carol Thomas

Illustrations by Holly Berry

JOANNA COTLER BOOKS
An Imprint of HarperCollins*Publishers*

The Bowlegged Rooster and Other Tales That Signify
Text copyright © 2000 by Joyce Carol Thomas
Illustrations copyright © 2000 by Holly Berry
Printed in the United States of America. For information address
HarperCollins Children's Books, a division of HarperCollins Publishers,
1350 Avenue of the Americas, New York, NY 10019.
www.harperchildrens.com

Library of Congress Cataloging-in-Publication Data
Thomas, Joyce Carol.
   The bowlegged rooster and other tales that signify / by Joyce Carol
Thomas ; illustrations by Holly Berry.
     p.   cm.
   Summary: From the time he is hatched, Little Rooster learns lessons of
life from his father and the other barnyard birds at Grandpa Goose's funeral,
Crow's wedding, and a Christmas celebration.
   ISBN 0-06-025377-0. — ISBN 0-06-025378-9 (lib. bdg.)
   [1. Roosters—Fiction.   2. Chickens—Fiction.   3. Birds—Fiction.]
I. Berry, Holly, ill. II. Title.
PZ7.T36696 Bo   2000   99-53291
[Fic]—dc21   CIP
                                             AC

Typography by Alicia Mikles
1 2 3 4 5 6 7 8 9 10
❖
First Edition

To Gloria Pecot, with love

—J.C.T.

About Tales That Signify

WHEN ANIMALS STAND in the place of people and playfully speak their minds, this is what I call signifying. The Bowlegged Rooster, the Bald-headed Buzzard, the Bullfrog Quartet, and that fiddle-playing Lizard remind us of what being fully human is all about. Our busy birds and their fantastic friends run up and down the barnyard, boasting and bragging, strutting and crowing, worrying and fretting. And making many mistakes along the way. What a delight to see Baby Rooster charming them and maybe even us into changing our sometimes selfish, sometimes foolish ways. We can open our hearts to humor and our minds to magic. And just like the signifying birds, we might get so tickled that we giggle, we grow, we wonder, we change.

—*Joyce Carol Thomas*

THE BOWLEGGED ROOSTER

NOW REGULAR HUMANS mistakenly think that at night all chickens just sit up on a perch in the henhouse and sleep deep sleep, guarding the nest like some kind of midnight chicken police. But this is not true. Especially not in Possum Neck, Mississippi, where in a

henhouse late one night, an egg rocked
to and fro—

quickety-quick-creak-creak

quickety-quick-creak—

impatient as the late spring wind.

"Let me . . . *quickety-quick* . . . outta
here!" peeped the biddy, creaking
inside the brown speckled shell.

The other biddies, snuggled in their
own nests, were trying to escape their
eggshells too, but they were quieter
about the thing.

Papa Rooster, standing on the side
of the chicken coop, his foot propped
up on the bench where his wife sat
sewing, looked in the henhouse window at that one egg quickening. He
shook his head and said, "One in every

bunch got more *ziggidy-zest*. Got to get going before the rest."

"How would you know, Papa Rooster?" asked Lizard, climbing high on the nearby fence.

"Of course, the reason he knows," clucked Mama Hen, "is because he's recognized someone just like him. Corn never falls too far from the stalk."

What she meant was, Rooster was always Rooster.

But as usual, Papa Rooster didn't pay her no mind.

All night long, he went up and down the barnyard, carrying on, fussing and signifying.

Papa Rooster said,

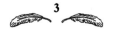

3

"Birds in the bush ask what
  comes first, the chicken or the egg.
Everybody in the barnyard
  wants to know.
Should've asked me—
I'd have told them long time ago,
'Course it was the rooster!"

Mama Hen didn't necessarily agree.
She jumped up and spoke her mind:

"Maybe that's true,
  According to you.
  Maybe you ought to think again,
  I think it was the hen."

Over on the rail, Lizard lifted his
head and said,

"Depends on where you've been
  Or what you used to."

Mama Hen and Papa Rooster just

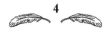

shook their tail feathers.

"I say it was the hen,"
chanted the hen.

"I think it was the rooster,"
ranted the rooster.

But they said no more just then.
The full moon was lighting up the
barnyard like nature's own night-light,
which it was. Now was the time when
the hens put on their aprons, cooked
corn pudding, corn bread, corn pone,
corn fritters, corn cakes, corn on the
cob, and corn off the cob.

And while the hens were cooking
and visiting, Papa Rooster called the
rooster men together. He lifted the
latch on Farmer Brown's cellar and led
the roosters to the cool jugs of apple

cider kept bubbling for special occa-
sions.

They drank the seasoned cider until
they were *burpity-burping* full. When
they came back to the barnyard, they
wobbledy-wobbled on fences and lifted
their stubby wings.

They were so full and happy they
thought they could take to the sky,
spread their wings—like falcons—and
fly.

Mama Hen took one look at her
husband and shook her head.

"Would you sit down and quit?"
she asked. "Papa, you can't fly. Don't
even try!"

"Grandpa Goose's getting buried in
the morning, and I'm going to fly to

the funeral," said Papa Rooster.

"Oh no, you ain't," said Mama Hen as she picked up the suit she was making for Papa Rooster and began to sew on the buttons. "You're going to walk just like everybody else."

"Walk? Why, in my younger days, I flew above the trees and through the clouds," bragged Papa Rooster.

Mama Hen put her hands on her hen hips and said, "I've been here as long as you and I haven't ever seen you breezing with the bats and the buzzards."

"Just keep sewing my costume," said Papa Rooster. "You know I got to show everybody out."

"One of these days that old pride'll get the best of you," said Mama Hen.

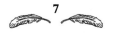

"Anyway, you ought to change your act. We got another little one coming, and I sure don't want this one taking after you! Prancing all over the farm, cock-a-doodle-dooing wheresonever you see fit. Can't find you when I need you half the time."

"Cock-a-doodle-doo!"
crowed Papa Rooster, his feathers a little ruffled. "Mamie Lou, over in the next chicken yard, doesn't share your misgivings about me."

"And I didn't either when you first came a-courting," said Mama Hen. "But a body gets tired of all this bragging. Hand me that red thread."

And Papa Rooster handed Mama the red thread for his rooster vest. She

was making it especially thick in the chest with turkey feathers and duck feathers in and all around it. She knew she didn't really need to put in any more padding.

Papa Rooster's chest was stuck out anyway, but Mama Hen had to admit, it tickled her to make him happy.

And when she had finished his costume, Papa Rooster was some satisfied. There were sequins and silver buttons all in a row, and the speckled red shirt and vest matched his comb.

Papa Rooster strutted

steppity-step-step-step

steppity-step-step

on those crooked bowlegs, long like stilts, the better to look over into everybody's nests and flirt with the fluffy hens.

Mama Hen said, "Husband, you look mighty handsome, if I have to say so myself."

"*Cock-a-doodle-doo!*"
crowed the rooster.

"*Oh, we will*
  cock-a-doodle-doo
  at the funeral. We will
  cock-a-doodle-doo
  till the sun drops down
  low in the graveyard."

"Shush your fooling now," said Mama Hen. "These babies need peace and quiet to come into this world."

She looked around at all the eggs lying in their nests, but she had her eye on her own special egg that rocked

quickety-quick-creak-creak

quickety-quick-creak

all around the other little biddies.

"Be quiet?" exclaimed Papa Rooster. "Not me. When I came into the world, there was a party going on, just for me, don't you know! And now, my little rascal's hatching, we have to put us on a show. Just for him!"

Papa Rooster was so excited about the new baby that he began to

steppity-step-step-step

steppity-step-step.

Just a–strutting and disturbing the gravel in the barnyard, dancing the Susie Flew, the Rabbit Foot, the Mule Cutback.

Papa Rooster's festive mood about the new baby was so contagious that Lizard started fiddling his fiddle. Then the bullfrogs in the Bullfrog Quartet joined in, crooning,

"Croakety-croak-croak-croak

Croakety-croak-croak."

"Come on now," cawed the crow to the eagle and the hawk flying high above the ground. "I do believe Papa Rooster's gonna push the dust around."

And the eagle and the hawk they

flappity-flew

on down.

Papa Rooster danced and *whirly-whirled* with such joy until that egg rocking

quickety-quick-creak-creak

quickety-quick-creak

felt the barnyard shaking from all that dancing.

In fact, Papa Rooster, with his fiddle-playing Lizard, and his Bullfrog Quartet, rocked the entire barnyard so hard that the henhouse started shaking and

quickety-quick-creak-creak

quickety-creak-creak

turned into a big

Quickety-CRACK!

And all of a sudden Baby Rooster came

steppity-step-stepping

steppity-step-step

out of his shell!

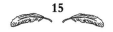

Everybody stopped dancing and playing and looked at the little biddy. Baby Rooster opened his eyes wide and said,

Peep.

A small sound.

Peep. Peep-peep.

The sound grew bigger.

Peep. Peep-peep-peep.

Then Baby Rooster cocked his head. "Where's the music, Papa?" he asked.

All the birds started cheering and Mama Hen clucked and Papa Rooster grinned.

The music started up again and Baby Rooster began to dance bow-legged.

"Just like his daddy," said Mama Hen with a happy shake of her head.

"Cock-a-doodle-doo!" Papa Rooster sang with pride. "Won't be long, he'll crow 'fore day too!"

"Crow 'fore day, uh-huh," said Mama Hen. "Just like his papa."

The music kept playing on through the night, and Baby Rooster *wiggledy-wiggled* between Papa Rooster and Mama Hen, who was shaking her tail feather every which way.

Soon Baby Rooster found himself in the center of a big circle, all the birds dancing around him in the moonlight. Everybody was so thrilled to see Baby Rooster dancing bowlegged and carrying on, they *whirly-whirled*

whirly-whirled

their wings and

cacklety-cacklety

cacklety-cacklety

the way birds do when they're happy.

Baby Rooster danced until sunup, when his papa let out a

"Cock-a-doodle-doo!"

And Baby Rooster looked up at his papa, and stretched himself as tall as he could get, and let out his very own little

"Cock-a-doodle-doo!"

And Papa Rooster clapped his wings together.

"Just like his daddy," Mama Hen said.

"Cock-a-doodle-doo!"

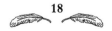

crowed Papa Rooster.

"*Cock-a-doodle-doo!*"

answered Baby Rooster.

Everybody laughed and cheered to
see father and son

steppity-step-strut-strut

steppity-step-strutting

and

cockle-a-doodle-dooing

as the sun came smiling up over the
barnyard.

GRANDPA GOOSE'S FUNERAL

NOW THAT THE sun had risen, it was time to go to Grandpa Goose's funeral.

"Time to go. Time to rise and fly," Papa Rooster called.

"Time to go. Time to rise and fly," Baby Rooster repeated.

He was dressed in an outfit just like

his daddy's, with silver buttons all in a row.

Mama Hen went to be with the other hens while Papa Rooster and Baby Rooster

steppity-step-step-stepped

steppity-step-stepped

their bowlegged way at the front of a long line of birds, all heading to Grandpa Goose's funeral to pay their last respects.

Above their heads, the air birds *whirly-whirled* through the sky, bound for Grandpa Goose's funeral too.

"We loved him so much," said Papa Rooster to Baby Rooster as they walked.

"Why did he die?" asked Baby Rooster.

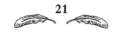

"He had lived a long, long time," explained Papa Rooster.

When they reached the graveside, Grandma Goose made room for Baby Rooster, who *wiggledy-wiggled* up under her and *snuggled* with the other little grandbaby goslings.

And Papa Rooster sat down with all the other menfolk.

As soon as everyone was settled, Miss Robin began to sing in her sweet voice, and everybody hummed along:

"Swing low, sweet chariot,
Coming for to carry me home.
I looked over yonder
And what did I see
Coming for to carry me home . . . "

Papa Rooster and all Grandpa

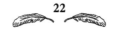

Goose's friends felt mighty sorrowful when they thought how sad life would be without kind and gentle Grandpa Goose.

Baby Rooster had never known Grandpa Goose, but he stroked Grandma Goose's feathers.

Everybody was crying as Miss Robin finished singing up the last verse:

> *". . . A band of angels coming*
>> *after me*
>
> *Coming for to carry me home."*

"How long were you and Grandpa Goose married?" Baby Rooster asked Grandma Goose.

"Till death did us part," said Grandma Goose, dabbing her eyes with a handkerchief.

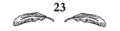

Papa Rooster murmured, "Married for life!" Then he leaned over to Baby Rooster and whispered, "Son, that's the way our friends the geese live. They take a vow for life."

"What's a vow, Papa Rooster?" asked Baby Rooster.

"A vow is a promise," said Papa Rooster. "When geese marry, they promise to stay together forever."

Now that the song was over, Baby Rooster wasn't sure what would happen next, but he saw his daddy talking with Crow. They seemed to be having a little misunderstanding.

"I wonder what's the matter," chirped Baby Rooster.

So he untucked himself from under

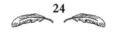

Grandma Goose's wing and *steppity-stepped* over to try to see what was going on.

"I should say the eulogy," cried Crow. "Why, when I was a little crowling, I sat on Grandpa Goose's knee. And I loved him the best!"

"And I loved Grandpa Goose with all my heart," Papa Rooster cock-a-doodle-dooed.

Just then Buzzard spoke up.

"No, I'm the one should deliver the eulogy," buzzy-buzzed Buzzard. "I loved him the most."

"No I did," caw-caw-cawed Crow.

Buzzard said, "Why, Crow, I'd do a good job of eulogizing. And Rooster, I'm a bigger bird than you are. I got presence."

"Now I'm the one with presence!" proclaimed Papa Rooster, sticking out his chest.

"What's presence?" asked Baby Rooster.

"Being able to speak before people," said Papa Rooster.

"Oh," chirped Baby Rooster, and he rubbed his chin as Papa Rooster, Crow, and Buzzard went back to arguing.

"I'll perform the eulogy," cock-a-doodle-dooed Papa Rooster.

"No, I'll say the eulogy," crowed Crow.

"No, I'll present the eulogy," buzzed Buzzard.

"What's a eulogy?" asked Baby Rooster.

They all stopped and looked at Baby Rooster.

"Why," explained Papa Rooster, "a eulogy is something you say in praise of a person."

"So he may rest in peace," cried Mama Hen, shaking her head at all the fussing men birds.

"Why can't everybody say the eulogy?" Baby Rooster peeped in a small voice.

Papa Rooster stopped his fussing and looked at his child.

"What did you say, Baby Rooster?" Papa Rooster asked.

Baby Rooster peeped a little louder.

"Why can't everybody say the eulogy?" he repeated. "All three. Buzzard, Crow, and you, Papa?"

Everybody was silent until Grandma Goose spoke up.

"I'd like that," she said.

Buzzard, Crow, and Papa Rooster looked at one another and nodded.

"We all loved him," they said together.

"That's the truth," said Papa Rooster. He asked Lead Bullfrog, "May we have a song, please?"

Before he began to sing, Lead Bullfrog said, "Grandpa Goose believed that love gives us wings." And then he signaled to Lizard, who tucked his fiddle under his fiddle chin and began playing a soft melody. The Bullfrog Quartet stood by the grave and lifted their voices in song:

> *"I got wings, you got wings*
> *All a God's children got wings*
> *When I get to heaven gonna*
>   *put on my wings*
> *Gonna fly all over God's*
>   *heaven . . ."*

Baby Rooster felt *fuzzy-wuzzy-warm* feelings of love as the wingless frogs sang about flying. Suddenly, Baby Rooster knew deep down that all God's creatures, even those without feathers, could have wings. Wings of love.

After the singing, Papa Rooster started the eulogy.

"Good birds of the air and the

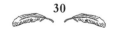

ground, *cock-a-doodle-doo* to you. It is our solemn duty to eulogize Grandpa Goose. Now Grandpa Goose was a kindly old soul. Went hungry some days because he wouldn't hurt a fly. Grandpa Goose was a legend in his own time."

Then Crow picked up the telling.

"Yes," gently cawed Crow. "Grandpa Goose was one of a kind. He found time to tell nursery rhymes to all the biddies."

"He would have loved to tell you a story, Baby Rooster," whispered Grandma Goose.

"He always said that all the winged creatures should get along," continued Buzzard. "Grandpa Goose believed that we're all perched here on earth, sharing the planet."

"And sometimes the sky," agreed Crow.

"Grandpa Goose wanted only peace in his barnyard," said Papa Rooster.

"What's peace?" asked Baby Rooster.

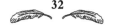

"Peace means no fussing," Mama Hen said, eyeing Papa Rooster.

"You mean like today?" asked Baby Rooster.

Mama Hen nodded and all the menfolk looked at the ground and coughed.

"Grandpa Goose believed all the birds in the barnyard should get along," Grandma Goose said.

Baby Rooster felt that *fuzzy-wuzzy-warm* feeling again. A sweet rhythm made his wings flutter and his feet move. He began to sing his own little song:

> *"Every bird who has a feather*
> *Must learn to live*
> *To live together."*

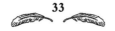

Grandma Goose put her arms around Baby Rooster and gave him a big hug for reminding them all what Grandpa Goose's life was about. Everybody began to sing Baby Rooster's song:

> *"Every bird who has a feather*
> *Must learn to live*
> *To live together."*

On the way home from the funeral, Papa Rooster, Crow, and Buzzard forgot about any misunderstanding. They thought about loving one another the way they had all loved Grandpa Goose. Everyone who had come to Grandpa Goose's funeral

> *steppity-step-step-stepped*
> *steppity-step-stepped*

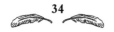

down the road and

    whirly-whirly-whirled

through the sky, singing Grandpa
Goose's praises and chanting Baby
Rooster's words:

> *"Every bird who has a feather*
> *Must learn to live*
> *To live together."*

THE BALD-HEADED BUZZARD

BACK HOME AT the barn-yard after Grandpa Goose's funeral, all the birds rested their wings. All the birds, that is, except for Buzzard, who glided

zoom, zoom, zoom

as he circled over and over again directly above Baby Rooster.

Baby Rooster looked up and said, "Papa, I know

> 'Every bird who has a feather
> Must learn to live
> To live together.'

But why does Mr. Buzzard keep buzzing over me?"

Papa Rooster raised his head and called, "What're you looking at, Buzzard?"

"At Baby Rooster's feathers," answered Buzzard in a sad, admiring voice.

"What about them?" asked Papa Rooster.

"They're the most wondrous things I have ever seen," said Buzzard.

"They do look some handsome,"

said Papa Rooster proudly.

"Thank you," chirped Baby Rooster.

"But Buzzard, tell me this, why are you looking so unhappy?" asked Papa Rooster.

Buzzard just came right on out with it. "It's 'cause I'm bald-headed," he said.

Buzzard's simple admission put everybody in a mood to help.

The tenderhearted hens clucked with pity and interest.

Every bird had a suggestion, but nobody had a solution until Crow stepped forward.

"What you need," cawed Crow, "is to go on down to the river and

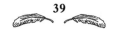

wash your head in its mighty stream

Every morning and

Every night

For seven days

And seven nights."

"A full week?" asked Buzzard.

"That's right," cawed Crow. "Why, before you know it, you'll wake up one morning and fine feathers'll be sprouting up through the top of your bald, bald head. Um-hmm."

"That so?" asked Buzzard, a hopeful smile brightening his gloomy face.

"But you got to talk a *loooong* time to the river," cawed Crow, feeling all-important with his advice.

"Talk a *loooong* time?" asked Baby Rooster. "Why?"

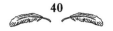

"Because it's a feather-asking ceremony," explained Crow. "And a feather-asking ceremony takes time."

"Seven days and seven nights! That *is* a long time," said Buzzard. "I'm gonna need me some help."

"I'll help," said Crow.

"We'll help," said the bullfrogs.

"I will too," said Lizard.

"And so will I," said Papa Rooster.

Baby Rooster chirped, "But Mr. Buzzard, why do you have such a bald head anyway?"

"Well, you see, Baby Rooster," said Buzzard, "a long time ago nobody had any feathers."

"Not a one?" asked Baby Rooster.

"Not a single one," answered

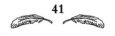

Buzzard. "Nothing covered our bones but skin. When the call came for everyone to go get them some feathers, I started out just like the rest. Then I saw some trash on the road, and I stopped to clean it up."

"Yes, that's his duty," Papa Rooster said to Baby Rooster.

"What's a duty?" asked Baby Rooster.

"A duty is a responsibility," explained Papa Rooster.

"And so you were taking care of your duty," Baby Rooster said to Buzzard.

"Yes, Baby Rooster, I was responsible," continued Buzzard. "As I worked picking up the litter, I was looking

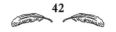

forward to my feathers. But by the time I finished cleaning up the road and got to where they were passing out feathers, they'd just about run out. Lucky for me, I got enough to cover my tail and my body. But not my head."

"Oh, my," said Baby Rooster, sympathy all in his voice.

"That's just like it happened," said Crow. "Everybody was all dressed up and looking at Buzzard right pitiful."

"Buzzard," said Crow, "just what kind of feathers would you like on your head?"

"I wouldn't mind having me some black ones like yours, Crow," Buzzard answered.

Crow cawed as he looked at his

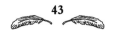

own feathers with pride. He was glad somebody wanted what he had.

"Or," continued Buzzard, as he looked at Baby Rooster, "I wouldn't mind having some white ones like you, Baby Rooster."

Baby Rooster preened just a little bit.

"Or," said Buzzard, "some red ones like yours, Papa Rooster."

"Of course you want the best," said Papa Rooster. "Now I don't let any and everybody copy the very thing that makes me unique. But for you, Buzzard, I'll make a special exception. You're welcome to go on down to the river and see about getting you some red feathers just like mine."

"Or just like mine," peeped Baby Rooster.

"Or just like mine," cawed Crow.

To make his point, Papa Rooster went up and down the fence

steppity-step-strut-strut

steppity-step-strutted,

showing off his sparkling plumage.

And Baby Rooster hopped up on the fence and pranced in step behind his daddy.

Steppity-step-strut-strut

Steppity-step-strut.

"You both look mighty fine," said Buzzard.

Papa Rooster and Baby Rooster took a bowlegged bow.

Then they went all over the barnyard

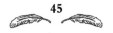

advertising the event.

"It's gonna be a big ceremony down by the riverside," said Papa Rooster.

"Big ceremony," peeped Baby Rooster.

Papa Rooster hitched up his trousers and added, "We're gonna request up some feathers for Buzzard's bald head."

"Feathers for Mr. Buzzard's bald head," chirped Baby Rooster.

Together Papa and Baby chanted,

"Every morning
And every night
For seven days
And seven nights."

"We'll be there," Lizard said.

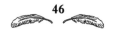

"We'll be there," promised Lead Bullfrog and his Bullfrog Quartet.

The next morning, at the crack of dawn, Papa Rooster cock-a-doodle-dooed.

And all the barnyard animals got up, dressed up, and started heading for the river.

When all were perched on logs and branches, Papa Rooster and Buzzard waded out into the river until the water came up to their knees.

Then Papa Rooster held up his wings for everybody to be quiet.

"O great river," began Papa Rooster.

"O great river," repeated Baby Rooster along with the rest of the

gathering of chickens, birds, lizards, and frogs.

"O great river," continued Papa Rooster, "we come before you in search of feathers for Brother Buzzard's head. Now he's a good buzzard. He always does his duty keeping our roads clean of garbage and other unseemly sights."

"That's the truth," called Mama Hen.

Papa Rooster continued, "Buzzard's set such a good example that we do our duty by picking up after ourselves too. I think you'd agree that he's earned the utter right to be here this sunrise, asking you for a heapful of feathers for his Buzzard head."

It was such a moving situation that all the hens dabbed at their eyes and patted Sister Buzzard on the shoulder.

Papa Rooster looked around solemnly at the crowd, then took hold of Brother Buzzard and dipped him over into the rushing waters of the river.

"Oh!" gasped all the birds.

As soon as Buzzard came up shaking his head in the sparkling sunrise, Lizard whipped out his fiddle and began playing. And the Bullfrog Quartet joined in and sang a hopeful song. They leaned their heads together on the riverbank and crooned so sweet even the songbirds nodded.

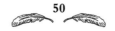

"Please, Mr. River,
  Make Buzzard handsome
  By giving him feathers
  For his bald, bald head
  Then he'll be beautiful
  And even more dutiful
  He won't be sad,
  but happy instead
  If you'd just give him feathers
  For his bald, bald head."

When they were finished singing, Buzzard peered over into the face of the river to see if he could detect any feathery sprouts on his head. But Papa Rooster told him it was too soon.

"Too soon?" asked Buzzard.

"Don't you remember what Crow said?" asked Papa Rooster.

And Baby Rooster chanted:

"Every morning
And every night
For seven days
And seven nights."

"That's right," said Papa Rooster, and he counted the days by scratching lines in the mud.

So, every morning and every night all the birds gathered together to watch Papa Rooster

dippity-dip dip

Buzzard's head in the

rippity-rip
rippity-rippling

river. And then every morning and every night, Buzzard looked into the mirror of the river, hunting for just a sign of sprouting feathers, but never finding even one.

Finally, on the seventh night, all the birds came together for the last time.

Papa Rooster
  cock-a-doodle-dooed
in his loudest, proudest rooster voice. Then he called out:

  "O mighty river
    The giver of fish
    to the birds of the air
    The giver of moisture
    to Lizard
    The giver of minnows
    to the bullfrogs
    Look up, o mighty river,
    you mighty giver,
    And give feathers for

Buzzard's bald head!"

Then Papa Rooster

dippity-dipped

Buzzard's head one last time.

Suddenly, everybody heard an earth-shaking noise. And they all looked up to the sky.

Nobody knew where the storm clouds had come from. But all of a sudden the thunder was rumbling and the lightning was flashing and the moon was hiding its face.

Everything and everybody trembled.

And then through the spattering hail and rain, the birds heard a mighty sound:

"Brother Buzzard!"

It was a voice that rocked the trees.

"You'd better be happy with the head I gave you."

Everybody gasped, and the voice continued.

"Brother Buzzard, unlike Rooster, you're already blessed with the gift of flight. Your head's designed bald on purpose, so there'll be no feathers in the way while you're cleaning up the roads."

"Now I understand," whispered Buzzard with a smile.

But the voice wasn't finished talking. It went on to address each and everyone present, letting the message sink into the minds of the listeners.

"All of you'd better be happy
with what you got,

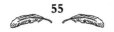

And heed every word I've said,
Or I'll take every feather
And leave you naked
as Buzzard's head."

The voice was so big that it scared Baby Rooster just a little, and he

steppity-stepped
quick-quick
steppity-stepped
quick

over and stood by Papa Rooster on the riverbank.

"In other words," boomed the voice, "everybody here had better be thankful for what you got, and *get the cricket out of my creek!*"

The chickens and birds, joined by Lizard and Bullfrogs, hurried away as fast as they could, with Baby Rooster

    steppity-stepping

    quick-quick

    steppity-stepping

    quick

ahead of everyone else.

    The flapping of wings,

    whirly-whirly-whirl-whirl,

    whirly-whirly-whirl

and the hurried *scurrying* of feet,

    steppity-step-step-step

    steppity-step-step

filled the air.

    And the voice of the river, vibrating

like a great rush of water,

    whoosh, whoosh, whoosh!

    whoosh, whoosh, whoosh!

pushed them on away from there.

For the next week, humble Buzzard and proud Papa Rooster flapped all over Possum Neck, Mississippi, in their feather suits.

They preached to anybody who'd listen about the amazing lesson they received that seventh night at the river. They chanted, along with the Bullfrog Quartet and fiddle-playing Lizard:

"Buzzard is a
Bald-headed Beauty
A handsome Chap
It's true
It's your duty
To celebrate
Your own beauty
That runs like a river."

And Baby Rooster repeated,

"That runs like a river."

And all the birds sang together,

"That runs like a river

through you."

When the song was finished, Baby Rooster admired the purposeful beauty of Buzzard's bald head. Then he looked down at his own skinny legs, and he

steppity-step-strut-strut

steppity-step-strutted

all up and down the barnyard, happy with his own feathers and his own bowlegged beauty.

CROW
JUMPS
THE BROOM

T WAS NOT long after Buzzard came to realize his bald head was already beautiful enough, that Crow announced he was getting married.

Crow was so happy about his bride-to-be that he invited all branches of his family to the wedding in Possum

Neck, Mississippi.

"*Caw-caw-caw*

Caw-caw-caw,"

proudly sang Crow.

Happy as he was, though, Crow needed all the support he could get.

He was nervous.

Crow and Papa Rooster caw-caw-cawed and cock-a-doodle-dooed near the henhouse window as they discussed Crow's upcoming marriage.

Baby Rooster listened to every word.

"Papa Rooster," cawed Crow, "I wonder if I'll make a good husband and good father."

"You know," said Papa Rooster, "I asked my grandpa the same thing on my wedding day. Maybe you should talk to yours."

"That's a good idea," said Crow, nodding his head.

Now, while Crow was talking to Papa Rooster, the bride was inside the henhouse getting fitted for her dress by Mama Hen.

"Who's got the lace?" clucked Mama Hen. She looked around at all the other hens sewing the bridesmaid dresses. The hens, needles in their mouths, threads going every which-a-way, bustled here, bustled there.

Bustle here, bustle there,
bustle, bustle everywhere.

Just as Mama Hen was wrapping the bride in the beautiful white lace,

she caught sight of the menfolk snooping around outside.

"Get away from this window. Shoo!" said Mama Hen. "Don't you know it's bad luck for the groom to see the dress before the wedding day?"

So Crow, Papa Rooster, and Baby Rooster

steppity-step-strut-strut

steppity-step-strutted

on over to the fence so they could
check on the Bullfrog Quartet.

"Bullfrog music ready for the wedding?" asked Papa Rooster.

The bullfrogs all nodded their heads
and began to hum along in harmony:

"Yes sir,

We're ready, ready, ready

Been steady, steady, steady

Singing all night long.

We're ready, ready, ready

For the wedding song!"

Papa Rooster danced a little jig
in delight and turned to say something to Crow about the wonderful
harmony of the bullfrogs, but there

was no Crow in sight.

"Now where did that Crow go?" wondered Papa Rooster.

"He was here and now he's gone," chirped Baby Rooster.

"I guess he's pretty nervous," Papa Rooster chuckled. "Nervous about jumping the broom."

"Why do people call it jumping the broom?" asked Baby Rooster.

"It's a tradition," said Papa Rooster. "Jumping the broom is what folks do when they get married."

"Where is the broom?" asked Baby Rooster. At the henhouse there had been a lot of fuss over the dresses, but Baby Rooster hadn't heard anybody mention a broom.

"Somebody has to make the broom," explained Papa Rooster. "It has to be a new broom."

Baby Rooster nodded his head even though he didn't quite understand.

"Folks get married, folks jump the broom," he chirped.

Then he gave a funny little jump followed by a

hoppity-hop-hop.

"Folks get married, folks jump the broom," croakety-croaked the Bullfrog Quartet in union. And they danced,

hoppity-hop-hop,

hopping along with Baby Rooster.

That little dance got a little laugh out of everybody.

Now the hens had finished making the gown and dresses for the bride and her bridesmaids, so they came out into the barnyard.

"It's time to weave the broom for the ceremony," clucked Mama Hen. "Baby Rooster, would you go pick the broom straw for the broom?"

"Yes, ma'am," said Baby Rooster, who was only too glad to help.

He went out into the broomweed field and

    pickety-pick-pick-picked
    pickety-pick-picked

the golden straws for the jumping broom that the bride and groom would use in the wedding ceremony.

"Thank you for helping," Mama

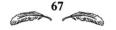

Hen clucked to Baby Rooster as he handed her a heap of broom straws.

"You're welcome," said Baby Rooster, so pleased to be appreciated.

Before long, the hens were bustling *busy, busy, busy* weaving a beautiful broom with curly ribbons on the handle.

Way after while, clouds of Crow's relatives and the beautiful bride-to-be's kinfolk began to arrive. They came *wheeling* and *cawing* out of the sky and started lining up in the trees.

The bride's family settled in on one side of the road.

The groom's family settled in on the other.

As far as Baby Rooster could see,

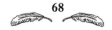

the trees were black with crows.

What a lofty sight! And what a glorious sound!

   "Caw-caw-caw-caw
   Caw-caw-caw,"
the crows cawed back and forth to one another.

There were so many crows, but nobody had seen tail nor feather of the groom. And it was almost time for the wedding!

"Now where could that Crow be?" Papa Rooster wondered out loud.

"Now where could that Crow be?" repeated Baby Rooster.

"Now where could that Crow be?" cawed the chorus of black birds from both sides of the road.

Nobody knew. But everybody sure was noisy about not knowing.

Caw, caw, caw, caw, caw!

It so happened that, while everybody was making a ruckus, Crow was over in the cornfield listening quietly to Grandpa Crow about how to be a good husband and father.

"Now you already know how to warn other crows when the farmer's trying to shoot," said Grandpa Crow. "And you're right to be loud about that. But when you come close to your own nest, you got to be silent. Don't want others to know where your nest is, and too, you don't want to disturb your family life. And when your wife is in the nest warming the eggs, you must feed her every day."

Crow listened respectfully to every word. He had no idea he was late to his own wedding!

Back at the barnyard, Papa Rooster and Baby Rooster kept nodding to all the barnyard creatures who kept pouring in from all over Possum Neck. They asked each guest,

"Where is Crow?
  Do you know?
  Do you know?
  Where is Crow?"

Finally, Crow made his appearance, all dressed up in his fancy tuxedo.

All the birds and barnyard creatures started cheering, and so Crow gave a low bow.

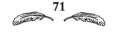

"Let's get this show on the road!" Papa Rooster called.

Grandpa Crow stepped up to officiate the ceremony, and Lizard started tuning up his fiddle.

Papa Rooster and Baby Rooster

steppity-step-strut-strutted

steppity-step-strut-strutted

over to the front row, where Mama Hen sat humming along to the music the Bullfrog Quartet was singing:

"Here comes the bride

Here comes the bride . . ."

Papa Rooster held Mama Hen's wing and squeezed it gently.

"Here comes the bride

Here comes the bride."

And Papa Rooster and Mama Hen

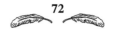

snuggled so close to each other on the bench that it made Baby Rooster smile. But he still managed to *wiggledy-wiggle* between the two of them.

Crow, in his black-and-white tuxedo, looked splendid. And the bride astonished them by her loveliness.

Grandpa Crow cleared his throat and began the official ceremony.

"Do you take this crow to be your lawful, wedded wife?" he asked Crow.

"I do," said Crow. And Crow's eyes were so bright with wonder that everybody sighed with joy.

"Do you take this crow to be your lawful, wedded husband?" Grandpa Crow asked the bride.

"I do," she said in a sweet whisper.

"Is it time to jump the broom?" Baby Rooster asked in the silence, and everybody laughed and cheered.

"Folks get married, folks jump the broom," Papa Rooster called out.

And that's just what Crow and his wife did.

As soon as their feet touched ground, Lizard struck up a tune on his fiddle. Crow led his bride onto the dance floor, where they danced beak to beak.

Baby Rooster stood watching this display of love, and then he turned to his mama and papa.

"Do you remember the day you got married?" he asked.

"Why, I remember our wedding

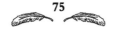

day just like it was yesterday," said Papa Rooster as he gazed into Mama Hen's eyes.

"And I do too," said Mama Hen.

"I was overflowing with so much joy, I thought the whole world was dancing," said Papa Rooster.

"The trees danced
The river danced
The sun, the sky, the wind
danced."

"Love must be a grand thing," peeped Baby Rooster.

"Yes, I do believe it is," said Papa Rooster, and he looked at Mama Hen with a blinding smile that outshone all his pride.

Baby Rooster looked down at his

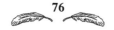

bowlegs and felt a little lost.

"Baby Rooster, come here. Do you know that you make our love shine even more?" said Papa Rooster and Mama Hen together.

They cuddled Baby Rooster close to them and pecked him on his little rooster chin. Baby Rooster felt all snuggly inside. The snuggly feeling went from his head down to his feet, and he started to dance to the lively tune Lizard was playing.

And the dancing felt so good he just couldn't help it. He skipped over and asked the bride to dance.

It was quite a sight: Baby Rooster dancing bowlegged, whirling the bride all up and down the barnyard. On the

sidelines, Crow clapped his wings, looking on with laughing eyes at the spry Baby Rooster.

And when Baby Rooster led Mrs. Crow back over to her husband so the two of them could continue the dance, Crow did a different jig. He started dancing bowlegged, just like Baby Rooster.

Soon all the barnyard creatures were lining up to dance bowlegged in a dance train behind the wedding pair. They all crooked their legs and

> *whirled around*
> *whirled around*
> *whirly-whirly-whirled around.*

Baby Rooster and Papa Rooster were tickled at how even unbow-

legged Lizard, the unbowlegged bullfrogs, and unbowlegged Buzzard
danced, pretending to be bowlegged
too.

Finally, all the chickens and birds
wished the newly wed couple well and
gave them their best wishes.

"Congratulations!" everybody called.

As Baby Rooster watched the bride
and groom fly off to a secret place for
their honeymoon, he saw how there
was so much joy that

> *The trees danced bowlegged*
> *The river danced bowlegged*
> *The sun, the sky,*
> *And even the wind danced*
> *   bowlegged.*

CHRISTMAS IN THE BARNYARD

I T WAS BABY Rooster's first Christmas.

All the fluffy chickens in the barnyard and birds in the air

cluckity-cluck-clucked

and

chirpity-chirp-chirped

"Merry Christmas, Baby Rooster!"

And Baby Rooster called "Merry Christmas" back, and watched the airbirds

whirly-whirl-whirl-whirl

whirly-whirl-whirl

through the sky, spreading cheer as they went, and looking forward to the Christmas celebration.

The sound of bells

ring-a-ling-a-ling-ling

ring-a-ling-a-ling

softened the air like the slow-falling snowflakes.

Baby Rooster and his little friends

skippity-skip-skipped

skippity-skip-skipped

along the white ground.

"Why don't we make a snow goose?" chirped Baby Rooster.

"Yes, let's!" the other biddies piped with excitement.

"First we'll need three big snow-balls," shouted Baby Rooster as he and the others packed snow firmly between their feathery fingers.

They *rolly-rolled* snow into the first snowball for the bottom part of the goose.

They *rolly-rolled* snow into the second snowball for the middle.

And they *rolly-rolled* the snow into the third snowball for the goose's head.

"Now for the buttons," said Baby Rooster, picking acorns off the ground.

He placed the acorn buttons in a line dotting them from the snow goose's

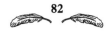

chest on down to his snowy waist.

For the snow goose's eyes, Baby Rooster used two black shiny stones, gleaming like ebony.

"Let me help!" said Papa Rooster, who had been watching from the hen-house. He picked up a curved twig that had fallen from a nearby cypress tree, and it became the goose's grin.

"Now that's a happy snow goose!" said Papa Rooster.

"What beautiful snow," said Baby Rooster, looking around the barnyard.

Mama Hen, who had come out to watch too, said, "We don't usually get a white Christmas this far south."

"Getting a snowy winter," said Papa Rooster. "I wonder what other wondrous gifts we'll get this Christmas."

Mama Hen gave Papa Rooster one of her mysterious looks, as if she was thinking deep, way back behind her eyes.

She clucked softly to herself,

"Cluck, cluck, cluck, cluck
Cluck, cluck, cluck."

But her clucking did not give one

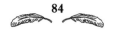

clue about what gifts Papa Rooster might expect for Christmas.

Both Papa Rooster and Baby Rooster had seen Mama Hen sewing endless streams of colorful cloth, reds and bright greens and sunny yellows and moon-flecked silvers. But she would hide the swatches the moment she saw Papa Rooster and Baby Rooster peek around the corner.

"Can't sneak up on Mama Hen and find out anything," fussed Papa Rooster to Baby Rooster. "Let's go sit a spell with Lizard."

And Papa Rooster and Baby Rooster started across the chicken yard,

steppity-step-step-step
steppity-step-step,

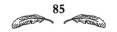

leaving their footprints in the snow.

When they reached Lizard, they saw he was busy decorating the snow-laden fence from rail to rail.

"What a sight!" said Papa Rooster as he admired the pine branches wrapped around the rails.

"Here," said Baby Rooster, handing Lizard some glossy holly leaves to add a festive green.

"Wonder what Mama Hen's getting me for Christmas?" said Papa Rooster as he handed Lizard more leaves.

"Probably something nice," said Lizard.

"I hope I get something nice too," said Baby Rooster as he watched Lizard wrap a piece of mistletoe around the last post.

Over to the side of the mistletoe post rested a big pile of gifts.

"Well, you all have a good day," said Lizard. "I got to finish putting cards on these Christmas presents."

As Papa Rooster and Baby Rooster started to step away from Lizard's rail, they leaned over and pretended they weren't looking for a package with

Rooster

scribbled on it. Their feathers *droopidy-droop-drooped* when they didn't see a single one.

"Come on, son, let's go pay a visit to the Buzzards," said Papa Rooster in a quiet voice.

Papa Rooster and Baby Rooster

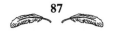

moseyed on over to where Mr. and
Mrs. Buzzard sat on the low, snow-
powdered limb of a fir tree, reading to
their little Buzzard babies.

"And she brought forth her
    firstborn son
And wrapped him in
    swaddling cloth
And laid him in a manger
Because there was no room for
    them in the inn . . ."

Mr. and Mrs. Buzzard paused and
looked at Papa Rooster and Baby
Rooster.

"Well, hello," Mrs. Buzzard said.
"Would you like to read with us?"

Baby Rooster nodded his head and
snuggledy-snuggled between the baby

Buzzards and listened to the rest of the story.

When the reading was finished, Papa Rooster said, "Well, thank you for sharing the story. We have to go pay our respects to the Crows. Come along, Baby Rooster."

While Papa Rooster spoke, he was stretching his neck and looking around in the Buzzards' tree limbs for something with his name on it.

And Baby Rooster was looking too. But they did not see even one gift that had

Rooster

scratched on it.

So Baby Rooster followed Papa Rooster

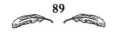

steppity-step-step-step
steppity-step-step
across the snow.

They found the newlywed Crows out in the middle of the barnyard getting the Christmas tree ready.

The Crows had brought their presents with them. And the presents were scattered near the tall pine tree where anybody could see the names that Crow's wife had carefully printed on them.

"Will you say a few words again this year at the Christmas party, Papa Rooster?" asked Crow as he roped a string of chestnuts on a high branch.

"I think so, Crow, but I don't know what to say," Papa Rooster answered.

"You'll think of something," said Crow.

"I hope so. Every time I start trying to practice my speech, the words go

tumbledy-tumbledy
tumbledy-tumbling

out of reach. You know what I mean?"

Crow said, "We love it when you speak, Papa Rooster. That is your gift to us and we look forward to it every year."

Baby Rooster listened to his father and Crow as he was squatting down reading the names on the Crows' packages, but he didn't see the word

Rooster,

big or little, written anywhere.

"Would you like to help decorate

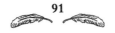

the tree, Baby Rooster?" Mrs. Crow asked.

Baby Rooster nodded his head and Mrs. Crow handed him a clump of popcorn and berries.

Baby Rooster began stringing the popcorn and red berries on the low-hanging branches of the fir tree.

The glow thrown from the winter sun made the cranberries sparkle bright against the snow-dusted pine needles.

"That looks wonderful," said Mrs. Crow.

"We'd better go check on the Robins now," said Papa Rooster.

And Papa Rooster and Baby Rooster

steppity-step-step-step

steppity-step-stepped

on over to the Robins' place.

Papa Rooster and Baby Rooster found Papa Robin looking out over the Christmas scene from his perch in the tree by the barn. Papa Robin was so happy, he chirped when he talked.

"Look, *chirp,* at what special food, *chirp*, the women are preparing, *chirp,* for Christmas dinner."

And Papa Rooster and Baby Rooster followed Papa Robin's gaze. They too admired the delicious cranberry sauce that Mrs. Robin was *bustling-busy* cooking for the holiday table.

All the hens *bustled busy.* They

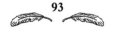

bustled here
bustled there
bustled busy everywhere

around the barnyard kitchen dressed in their red and green Christmas aprons.

As Papa Robin was busy talking about food and other kinds of gifts, Baby Rooster took a

peekity-peek-peek

at the Robins' pile of presents in a woven basket near the nest. He did not see his name among them.

But he didn't chirp a word about it.

And neither did Papa Rooster.

Just then they heard Lizard tuning up his fiddle.

"Time for the Christmas caroling," called Lizard.

Carrying the basket with his beak, Papa Robin flew down and joined Papa Rooster, Baby Rooster, and the chickens, birds, frogs, and lizards from all around as they gathered in the center of the barnyard.

"*Silent night*
Holy night,"
crooned the Bullfrog Quartet.

It was a night of peace, glittering with stars on the quilt of the new night sky.

Now here came the hens carrying candles in the moonlight. The scented candles flickered and bathed all their bird faces with a magical glow and perfumed the air with evergreen fragrance.

The hens held wings and walked in a circle around the pine tree, as Lizard and the bullfrogs continued singing.

They shaded the carol with notes of joy and chords of celebration:

"All is calm, all is bright
  Round yon virgin,
    mother and child
  Holy infant so tender and mild
  Sleep in heavenly peace . . .
  Sleep in heavenly peace."

Papa Rooster leaned back on his rooster claws and looked up at the stars and back down at the flock gathered all around.

Then he began his Christmas speech. "We are blessed to be here in our barnyard this special season, gifted with friends and relatives. These are the true gifts of Christmas."

"The true gifts of Christmas," Baby Rooster and the crowd chanted.

"A long time ago, a child was born," Papa Rooster continued.

"A child was born," called the gathering.

"And when he came into this world it was given that he was embraced by all kinds of barnyard creatures. All manner of creatures came from far and near to bring their gifts of welcome."

"To bring their gifts of welcome," echoed the crowd.

"And the child grew to know all their strengths and weaknesses," continued Papa Rooster. "And he abided

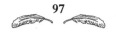

them. Just as he abides ours today. He loves us all. Chickens, crows, buzzards, geese, robins, lizards, and bullfrogs."

Papa Rooster looked around at all his feathered friends and family.

"And just think, this same child was born in a place very much like our barnyard right here in Possum Neck, Mississippi."

The listeners all nodded their heads, and Papa Rooster continued, "Perhaps it was to remind us all that to be humble is a blessing, even for those of us who find it hard to be humble."

"To be humble," murmured Baby Rooster and all within the sound of Papa Rooster's voice.

Papa Rooster looked up again at the clear night sky.

Then he looked at his gathering of friends and said, "I thank you for allowing me to share these Words of Christmas at this ceremony, year after year after year. And I thank you for the gifts that you give me every day of my life."

Each one nodded, silently reflecting for a good, long while.

Then Mama Hen fluttered her feathers, and lifted one wing finger. It was the signal that the rest of the gift giving could begin.

All the brand-new baby birds lined up in a row and accepted their gifts of toy nests and doll birds and play feathers.

The Bullfrogs gave Lizard rosin for his fiddle, rosin they had collected as sap from the pine trees.

The golden rosin, so nice and sticky, always made Lizard's bow cling to the strings, so the bow could fly across the fiddle with such agility that it seemed he had easy oil in his lizard elbow.

And Lizard gave the Bullfrogs glittery gloves that he had made special with sequins he had borrowed from Mama Hen's sewing collection.

The Bullfrogs

wiggledy-wiggledy-wiggled

the snug, warm gloves on their four bullfrog hands.

And Papa Rooster gave Mama Hen

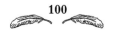

a little basket that he had tightly woven from tender reeds. Baby Rooster had found tiny acorns, which he had colored before tucking them inside.

"Oh, my! A button basket!" chirped Mama Hen, who gave them both a big hen hug. She was so delighted, she passed her gift around for all to admire.

Finally, Mama Hen reached way back up under the tree, where a pile of gifts was hidden from sight, and brought out Papa Rooster and Baby Rooster's gifts.

Everybody watched. Surprise and then joy spread across Papa Rooster and Baby Rooster's faces as they opened their presents.

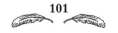

"Cock-a-doodle-doo!"

exclaimed Papa Rooster as he held up his new suit.

"Chirp! Chirp! Chirp!"

peeped Baby Rooster as he admired his new suit.

Every creature in the barnyard had chosen a swatch of cloth to make a special gift for Papa Rooster and Baby Rooster.

On the vests Mama Hen had embroidered birds, including a crow, a buzzard, a goose, and a robin. And she remembered the lizard and the bull-frogs too.

Quickety-quick

Papa Rooster and Baby Rooster put on their brand-new Christmas suits and strutted

    steppity-step-strut-strut

    steppity-step-strut

all up and down and around the barn-yard, dressed in all their Christmas humility.

Then they said proudly as all lent an ear,

    "Merry Christmas to every

        feathered and

        unfeathered one here.

    And we wish you all a Happy

        New Year."